# Letterland

D0994815

# New jeans

056 7794176

One Tuesday afternoon, Max went to Nick's house to play. Nick had on his new blue jeans.

Nick and Max went up to Nick's room.
"What do you want to do?" asked Nick.
"You choose."

First they drew some little pictures. Then
they drew a huge picture of a rocket
zooming into space.

"Now let's make a rocket!" said Max.
"I've got lots of boxes and tubes
we can use and a new pot of glue,"
said Nick.

Nick got the boxes and tubes and Max got
some old newspapers.
"We must not get glue on the carpet,"
said Max.

"No," said Nick opening the new pot of
glue and putting it on the stool.
"I must make sure I don't get glue on my
new jeans," he said.

Nick and Max glued some of the big tubes together to make the rocket. Nick made sure he did not get the glue on his new blue jeans.

"Let's glue on a few of these tubes to make the rocket boosters," said Nick.

"Then we could paint it all blue," said Max.

So Nick got a tube of blue paint and Max
helped him to paint the rocket. Nick made
sure he did not get blue paint on his new
jeans.

Soon their rocket was finished.
"It looks just like the one we drew!"
said Max.

Then Nick stepped back to look at the
rocket. But he stepped on the tube of blue
paint and paint went shooting across
the room.

"Oh no!" cried Max. He ran to help
Nick, but as he ran he knocked over
the stool.

The pot of glue flew across the room.
"Oh no!" cried Max.

Nick looked at his new jeans.
"It's okay!" he said with a grin. "There is
no glue or blue paint on my new jeans!"
"That's true!" said Max. "But …

"… just look at your room!"

"Oh no!" cried Nick.